# Home

## A JOURNEY THROUGH AMERICA

ILLUSTRATED BY

### Thomas Locker

EDITED BY THOMAS LOCKER AND CANDACE CHRISTIANSEN

VOYAGER BOOKS

HARCOURT, INC.

SAN DIEGO   NEW YORK   LONDON

*To Miriam Suzanne*

"Once by the Pacific" from THE POETRY OF ROBERT FROST EDITED BY EDWARD CONNERY LATHEM, © 1956 by Robert Frost, Copyright 1928, © 1969 by Henry Holt and Company, Inc. Reprinted by permission of Henry Holt and Company, Inc. "Gold" copyright © 1998 by Pat Mora. Excerpt from "Fog" in CHICAGO POEMS, copyright 1916 by Holt, Rinehart and Winston, Inc. and renewed 1944 by Carl Sandburg, reprinted by permission of Harcourt Brace & Company. "The River" copyright © 1998 by Jane Yolen reprinted by permission of Curtis Brown, Ltd. "Children of the Sky" copyright © 1998 by Joseph Bruchac. "Tree" copyright © 1998 by Eloise Greenfield. From "Song of a People" by Merle Good, copyright © 1993 by Good Books. Reprinted by permission of Good Books. "Birches in the Fall" copyright © 1998 by Thomas Locker.

www.harcourt.com

First Voyager Books edition 2000
*Voyager Books* is a registered trademark of Harcourt, Inc.

The Library of Congress has cataloged the hardcover edition as follows:
Home: a journey through America/[compiled and illustrated by] Thomas Locker.
p.   cm.
Summary: An anthology of poetry and prose by such writers as Carl Sandburg, Willa Cather, and Robert Frost, all celebrating aspects of the American landscape.
1. Landscape—United States—Literary collections.  2. Children's literature, American.
[1. Landscape—Literary collections.]  I. Locker, Thomas, 1937—
PZ5.H749  1998
810.8'032—dc21    97-18206
ISBN 0-15-201473-X

ISBN 0-15-202452-2 pb        H G F E D C B A

## Introduction

HOME is more than just the place we return to after being away. Home is something that becomes part of us as we live in it. For artists and writers, home can become part of how we see the world and how we shape our words or our artwork. For everyone, the place we call home becomes a part of our lives.

For the past ten years I have lived in the Hudson River valley of New York. I can see the river and the Catskill Mountains from my studio, and I often go out on foot with my easel and paint box to see trails and cliffs and waterfalls. Most of my paintings are landscapes—what other artists consider background is the focus of my work, and my favorite subject is the Hudson River valley—my home.

For *Home: A Journey through America*, Candace Christiansen and I have selected writings and commissioned poems from writers with individual and personal ways of seeing and describing the landscape where they make their homes. From the seacoasts to the plains to the desert, this collection of poems, prose, and blessings defines what home is to many of us. I have had the pleasure of creating artwork for these words. It is my hope that this book will present a vision of our varied and special land, and that *Home* will inspire readers to celebrate the special places they call home.

—T. L.

# From *Once by the Pacific*

ROBERT FROST

The shattered water made a misty din.
Great waves looked over others coming in,
And thought of doing something to the shore
That water never did to land before.
The clouds were low and hairy in the skies,
Like locks blown forward in the gleam of eyes.
You could not tell, and yet it looked as if
The shore was lucky in being backed by cliff,
The cliff in being backed by continent. . . .

*Robert Frost was born in San Francisco and lived in
California as a child, before moving to New England,
where he lived most of his life. He is one of America's
most beloved poets.*

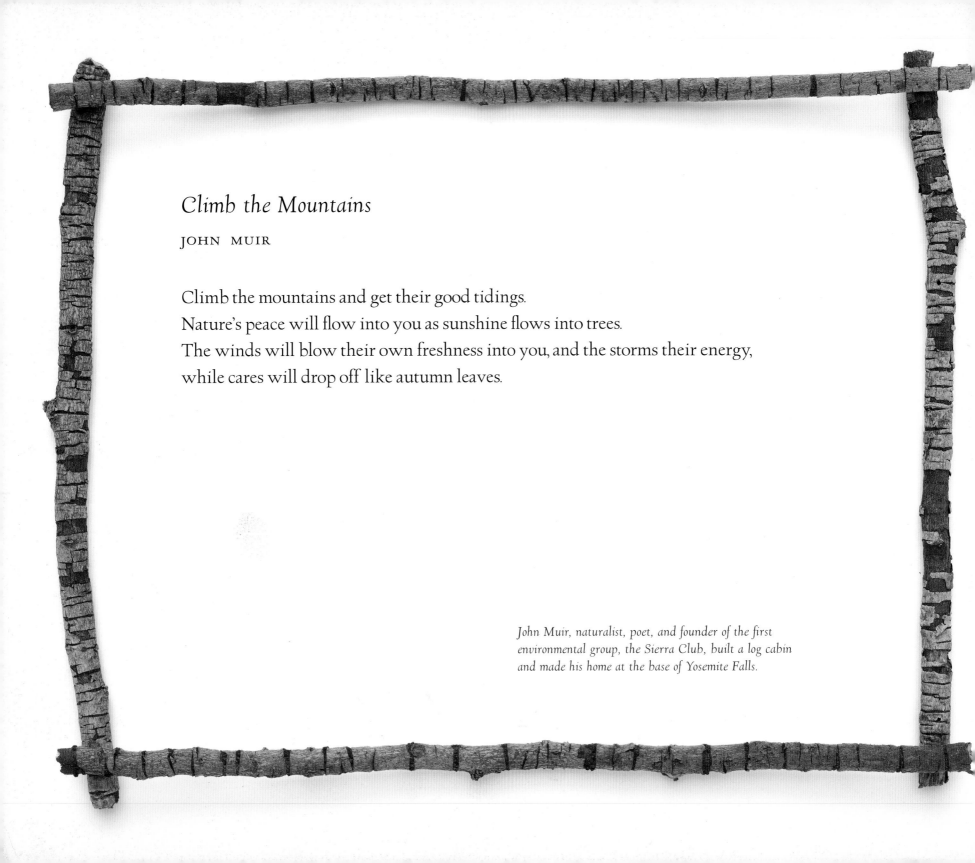

## Climb the Mountains

JOHN MUIR

Climb the mountains and get their good tidings.
Nature's peace will flow into you as sunshine flows into trees.
The winds will blow their own freshness into you, and the storms their energy,
while cares will drop off like autumn leaves.

*John Muir, naturalist, poet, and founder of the first
environmental group, the Sierra Club, built a log cabin
and made his home at the base of Yosemite Falls.*

# Gold

PAT MORA

When Sun paints the desert
with its gold,
I climb the hills.
Wind runs round boulders, ruffles
my hair. I sit on my favorite rock,
lizards for company, a rabbit,
ears stiff in the shade
of a saguaro.
In the wind, we're all
eye to eye.

Sparrow on saguaro watches
rabbit watch us in the gold
of sun setting.
Hawk sails on waves of light, sees
sparrow, rabbit, lizards, me,
our eyes shining,
watching red and purple
      sand rivers stream down the hills.

I stretch my arms wide as the sky
like hawk extends her wings
in all the gold light of this, home.

*Pat Mora, a poet and author, has spent many years
living in the Southwest desert.*

# From *My Ántonia*

WILLA CATHER

As I looked about me I felt that the grass was the country, as the water is the sea.
The red of the grass made all the great prairie the colour of wine-stains, or of certain
seaweeds when they are first washed up. . . . I felt motion in the landscape; in the fresh,
easy-blowing morning wind, and in the earth itself, as if the shaggy grass were a sort
of loose hide, and underneath it herds of wild buffalo were galloping, galloping. . . .
The light air about me told me that the world ended here: only the ground and sun
and sky were left, and if one went a little farther there would be only sun and sky. . . .

*Willa Cather grew up in Nebraska. Many of her books
are set on the midwestern prairie.*

# Fog

CARL SANDBURG

The fog comes
on little cat feet.
It sits looking
over harbour and city
on silent haunches
and then moves on.

*Carl Sandburg made his home in Chicago and wrote
about both the rural land and the industrialized cities
of the Midwest.*

# The River

JANE YOLEN

This slow river,
clean enough
for sweet salmon
to run its course again,
snakes through
greening grass banks
unstartled by spring.

We cross
macadam bridges,
River Road
to River Road,
over a millennium
of winding water
never getting wet.

Is progress counted
in the distance
we travel
or the distance
we still have to go?

*Jane Yolen lives one long block from the Connecticut River,*
*where River Road in her town of Hatfield, Massachusetts,*
*looks over the water to River Road in Hadley, Massachusetts.*
*She is the author of more than two hundred books for children*
*and adults.*

# Children of the Sky

JOSEPH BRUCHAC

Winds whisper
across the Comanche prairie,
A breathless chant
between promise and prayer.

We are alive
    we are alive.

Bluebonnets answer,
bowing their heads
toward the billowing clouds,
the slow song of the sky.

We are alive,
    we are alive.

White birds of power
soon will open their wings
bring rain to thirsty earth again,
sweet as the sight of home
to a traveler's eye.

We are alive,
    we are alive,
      we are all
        the children of the sky.

*Joseph Bruchac, a poet and storyteller, wrote this poem
after traveling through the area of Texas that is the home
of the Comanche Indian people. The poem is based on their
traditional understanding of that place, the land, the plants,
and earth and sky.*

# *Tree*

ELOISE GREENFIELD

Tree stands on storied ground,
like its brothers and sisters
in cities and towns.
listens. hears life.
weaves voices in its limbs.

cascades songs and tears and laughter,
new and old sounds overlapping.
Tree stands on storied ground,
rippling its leaves to the rhythms
of home.

*Eloise Greenfield, poet and author, was born in Parmele,
North Carolina. There she lived on a tree-lined street,
as she does today in Washington, D.C.*

# My Childhood's Home

ABRAHAM LINCOLN

My childhood's home I see again,
    And sadden with the view;
And still, as memory crowds my brain,
    There's pleasure in it too.
O Memory! thou midway world
    'Twixt earth and paradise,

Where things decayed and loved ones lost
    In dreamy shadows rise,
And, freed from all that's earthly vile,
    Seem hallowed, pure, and bright,
Like scenes in some enchanted isle
    All bathed in liquid light....

*Abraham Lincoln was president of the United States during the Civil War. His speeches and essays, including the Gettysburg Address, Thanksgiving Proclamation, and Emancipation Proclamation, represent some of the finest writings of that time. Abraham Lincoln's childhood home was in Spencer County, Indiana.*

## Song of a People

MERLE GOOD

We watch the past
create the now—
And wish to plant
before we plow—
We hear "goodbye"
in each hello—
And wish to stay
When we must go—

We try to catch
the closing door—
And seek for peace
in time of war—
As day makes night
a fugitive—
The living dream,
the dreaming live.

*Merle Good has written numerous books about Amish heritage. His poem exemplifies the tradition of blessings that exists in many American cultures, which includes meal blessings, house blessings, congregational blessings, and gathering blessings. He lives near an Amish community in Lancaster, Pennsylvania.*

# Birches in the Fall

THOMAS LOCKER

In the forests of New England
silver birch
lean left and right
turning, twisting
upward toward the light.

Although October maples
become an outrageous sight,
they hardly hold a candle
to the birch bark's
gleaming white.

*Thomas Locker has lived in Washington, Connecticut, and
now makes his home in the Hudson River valley of New York.*

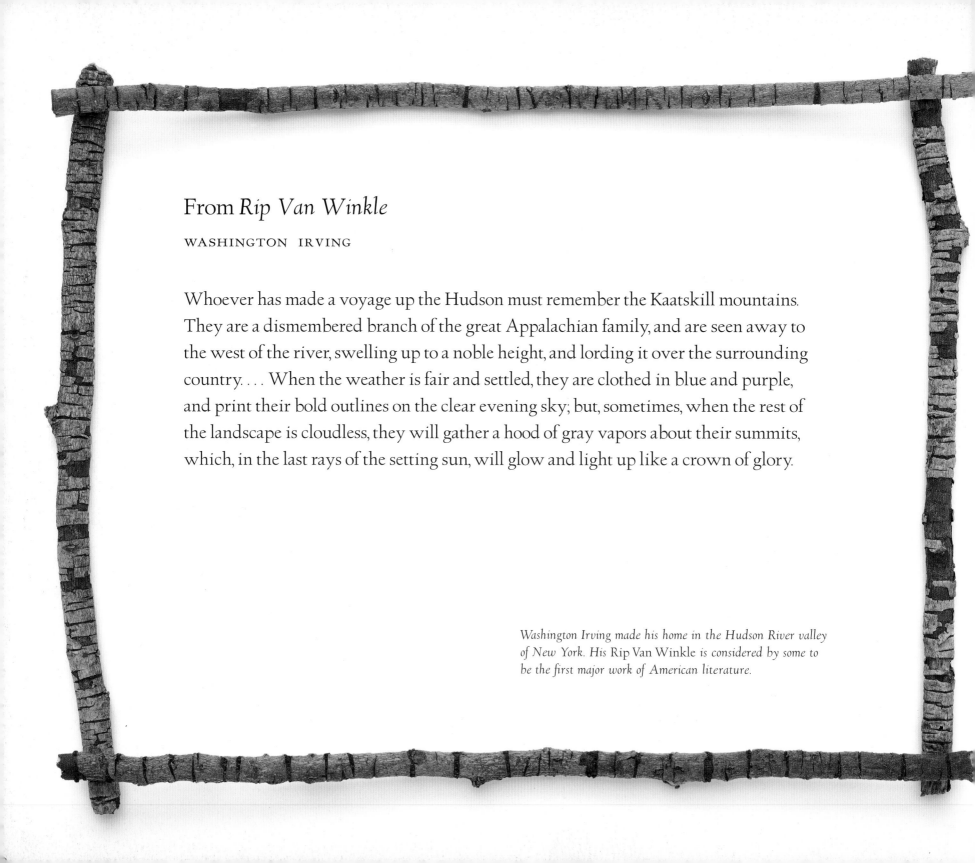

# From *Rip Van Winkle*

WASHINGTON IRVING

Whoever has made a voyage up the Hudson must remember the Kaatskill mountains. They are a dismembered branch of the great Appalachian family, and are seen away to the west of the river, swelling up to a noble height, and lording it over the surrounding country.... When the weather is fair and settled, they are clothed in blue and purple, and print their bold outlines on the clear evening sky; but, sometimes, when the rest of the landscape is cloudless, they will gather a hood of gray vapors about their summits, which, in the last rays of the setting sun, will glow and light up like a crown of glory.

*Washington Irving made his home in the Hudson River valley of New York. His Rip Van Winkle is considered by some to be the first major work of American literature.*

# From the *Journal*

HENRY DAVID THOREAU

Every day a new picture is painted and framed, held up for half an hour,
in such lights as the Great Artist chooses, and then withdrawn,
and the curtain falls.
And then the sun goes down, and long the afterglow gives light.
And then the damask curtains glow along the western window.
And now the first star is lit, and I go home.

*Henry David Thoreau is considered one of the first
environmentalists. He lived in a cabin he built on the
shore of Walden Pond, near Concord, Massachusetts,
and wrote this passage on January 7, 1852.*

PACIFIC
OCEAN

WA

AK

OR

ID

MT

ND

MN

SD

WY

NE

IA

NV

RED CLOUD
Cather's
*My Ántonia*

SAN FRANCISCO
Frost's
"Once by the Pacific"

UT

CO

M

YOSEMITE FALLS
Muir's
"Climb the Mountains"

KS

CA

AZ

SANTA FE
Mora's "Gold"

OK

HI

NM

NORTHERN TEXAS
Bruchac's
"Children of the Sky"

TX

N
W    E
S

LAKE SUPERIOR

WI

LAKE HURON

LAKE MICHIGAN

MI

IN

ICAGO dburg's iog"

IL

KY

TN

AL

MS

GA

FL

GULF OF MEXICO

LAKE ONTARIO

NY

LAKE ERIE

HUDSON RIVER VALLEY
Irving's *Rip Van Winkle*

PA

LANCASTER
Good's "Song of a People"

OH

SPENCER COUNTY
Lincoln's
"My Childhood's Home"

WV

VA

NC

SC

NJ

MD

DC

DE

ME

VT

NH

MA

CT

RI

WALDEN POND
*Thoreau's Journal*

HATFIELD, MA
*Yolen's "The River"*

WASHINGTON, CT
Locker's
"Birches in the Fall"

PARMELE, NC
Greenfield's "Tree"

ATLANTIC OCEAN

# WRITERS in this BOOK

Joseph Bruchac, born 1942
Saratoga Springs, NY

Willa Cather, born 1873
Winchester, VA

Robert Frost, born 1874
San Francisco, CA

Merle Good, born 1946
Lititz, PA

Eloise Greenfield, born 1929
Parmele, NC

Washington Irving, born 1783
New York, NY

Abraham Lincoln, born 1809
Larue County, KY

Thomas Locker, born 1937
New York, NY

Pat Mora, born 1942
El Paso, TX

John Muir, born 1838
Dunbar, Scotland

Carl Sandburg, born 1878
Galesburg, IL

Henry David Thoreau, born 1817
Concord, MA

Jane Yolen, born 1939
New York, NY

The illustrations in this book were done in oils on canvas.
The text type was set in Goudy Village.
The display type was hand lettered by Georgia Deaver.
Map by Georgia Deaver
Color separations by Bright Arts, Ltd., Hong Kong
Printed by South China Printing Company, Ltd., Hong Kong
This book was printed on 128 Japanese matte paper.
Production supervision by Ginger Boyer
Designed by Michael and Ryan Farmer